I0621209

FADING SHADOWS

LOVE BEYOND THE NIGHT

JOCELYN GEIGER

Fading Shadows

Copyright © 2024 by Jocelyn Geiger.

All rights reserved. No part of this publication may be reproduced, distributed, or transmitted in any form or by any means, including photocopying, recording, or other electronic or mechanical methods, without the written consent of the publisher. The only exceptions are for brief quotations included in critical reviews and other noncommercial uses permitted by copyright law.

MILTON & HUGO L.L.C.
4407 Park Ave., Suite 5
Union City, NJ 07087, USA

Website: *www. miltonandhugo.com*
Hotline: *1- 888-778-0033*
Email: *info@miltonandhugo.com*

Ordering Information:
Quantity sales. Special discounts are granted to corporations, associations, and other organizations. For more information on these discounts, please reach out to the publisher using the contact Information provided above.

Library of Congress Control Number: 2024908024
ISBN-13:   979-8-89285-067-4   [Paperback Edition]
                  979-8-89285-068-1   [Hardback Edition]
                  979-8-89285-066-7   [Digital Edition]

Rev. date: 05/14/2024

CHAPTER

1

BATTLING OBSESSIVE THOUGHTS: A MUTUAL STRUGGLE

In the realm of routine at the retail store, I, Mary, find solace in stocking items and managing the opening and closing shifts. My social life is confined to the walls of my house. One ordinary day, while working in aisle 4, a simple inquiry about sugar leads to a brief encounter. Guiding the person to aisle 6, a spark of interest ignites within me. Continuing to aisle 5, thoughts linger, and a box of Skittles slips from my hands. Surprisingly, the one who inquired about sugar assists me, and in that moment, my world shifts. Caught off guard, I sit up, a luxurious smile gracing my flushed cheeks, captivated by someone who has piqued my interest for the first time in 15 years. In that moment, a strange thought crossed my mind – was this person following me? However, reason prevailed; it was just an uncanny coincidence. Wanting to ease the potential awkwardness, I struggled to find words. Thankfully, the person spoke first, returning the dropped Skittles. I thanked them with a smile but couldn't help bursting into laughter, a nervous reaction to the unexpected encounter. Apologizing for my clumsiness, I was met with understanding as the person shared that, for a brief moment, I had brought color into their life. Touched by the person's sweetness, I found myself staring, unable to contain my admiration. Breaking the silence, I asked, "What is your name?" while continuing my stocking duties. The person replied, "My name is Hooshi." I smiled and, attempting a guess, said, "Hooshi, let me guess, Chinese?" Hooshi corrected me, revealing they were Vietnamese. My mind briefly wandered to Pearl Harbor, but I quickly realized the historical distinction. Hooshi, curious, asked about my name and tenure at Wally World. I shared, "I'm Mary, and I've been working here for 8 years." Moving to aisle 6, I found Hooshi still by my side. Unexpectedly, she asked, "Mary, would someone like you want to have dinner with me?" Panic set in as I stacked items, questioning why she found interest in me. In a whirlwind of thoughts, I wondered why I was being asked out. Hooshi sensed my unease, asking if I was okay. After a brief internal struggle, I nervously chuckled and assured her I was fine. Hooshi, considerate, mentioned I didn't have to agree. Before she could finish, I blurted out, "Yes, I'm interested." A genuine smile from Hooshi brought back the warmth between us. Completing the aisle, Hooshi asked for my number. I requested a pen and paper, and she promptly provided them. Scribbling down my address and a meeting time, I handed it to Hooshi. Unbeknownst to her, my nature tended toward obsession and control. Hooshi, perceiving it as a test, questioned her worthiness and punctuality, oblivious to my true intent. Hooshi departed, and as the assistant manager, I wrapped up work later than others. In the process, someone dashed in, snatching my bag. Distraught, I screamed, feeling the shock of an unexpected and distressing incident. Unaware that Hooshi was waiting in the parking lot, I was startled when she approached. In my panic, I didn't recognize her, and I reacted by hitting her until she revealed her identity. Overwhelmed with guilt and emotion, I collapsed, crying on the ground. Hooshi knelt beside me, embracing me in a comforting hug. Curious, I questioned why she was still there, and she explained she wanted to ensure I had a way home.

Sharing that she took the bus every day, I marveled at life's quirks. Hooshi kindly escorted me home, displaying an old-fashioned charm by opening the passenger door. As our eyes met, an intimate connection rushed between us. I hesitated, inviting her inside, but Hooshi declined, choosing to wait outside and smoke a cigarette. Outside, Hooshi battled self-doubt, questioning if I would like her, fearing I might find her actions at the store creepy. In her mind, doubts about her own interestingness and humor lingered. Unbeknownst to me, Hooshi struggled with obsessive thinking. As I stepped outside, Hooshi, awestruck, dropped her cigarette, fixating solely on me. She quickly regained composure, offering a compliment. I, on the other hand, began questioning my appearance, wondering if I looked ugly. Before I could answer myself, Hooshi approached, reassuring me that I was gorgeous and insisting on taking a picture, a moment that we both found a bit corny but chuckled about together. I found it easy to connect with Hooshi; being herself made everything effortless.

CHAPTER

2

UNEXPECTED CONFESSIONS AND UNSPOKEN FEARS

Hooshi graciously opened the car door, leading us to a special place – "Look and Eat," a beach-view restaurant. Concerned about the cost, Hooshi reassured me as we took our seats with a stunning view. She playfully remarked, "I'm glad I could blow," bringing a smile to my face. While waiting to order, I admitted it had been years since my last date. Hooshi, in jest, questioned if it was a date, momentarily causing me to blush. As the evening unfolded, I opened up about my past and the difficulty of finding understanding love. Surprised, Hooshi, wiping her mouth, couldn't believe someone like me had been single for so long. Curious about Hooshi's profession, I asked, and a brief hesitation followed, hinting at a deeper story. Hooshi, cautiously, asked if I'd run away upon learning more. In that moment, I assured her that I'd stay grounded with her. As Hooshi opened her mouth to speak, a mysterious figure in an all-black suit approached, whispering in her ear. My worry heightened, wondering what I had gotten into. Smirking at me, Hooshi hesitated but then revealed, "This is my restaurant." I was in shock, trying to process the unexpected revelation. Hooshi clarified, sharing that she earned money by selling things and doing favors. Shrugging off the revelation, I asked her what she thought I would like to eat. Hooshi, relieved that I didn't delve deeper into her mysterious life, suggested crab salad tacos, and I agreed. Leaving for the restroom, I pondered the situation. In the mirror, I questioned my choices and the perceived danger in Hooshi's demeanor. Returning to the table, Hooshi caught me off guard, asking if everything was okay. Smiling, I assured her, and we continued to enjoy our meal and laughter. However, when someone walked by, eyeballing Hooshi, my suspicions grew. Unable to contain my curiosity, I asked Hooshi about the encounter. Reluctantly, she revealed a shocking truth – she had shot the person's brother, and he held a grudge. I laughed, struggling to believe I was on a date with someone who might be a murderer, a perspective I hadn't considered about Hooshi. Amid the laughter, I couldn't believe Hooshi's revelation – "I shot his brother."

Pausing, I took a sip of water and whispered, "You killed someone?" Hooshi, finding my reaction cute, admitted with a smile, "I killed someone." Surprisingly, I didn't feel scared; there was an inexplicable assurance about Hooshi. Wanting to understand, I asked why, and her answer was chilling – she was paid to do it. I cautiously whispered, "Are you an assassin?" Hooshi confirmed, adding that it involved various tasks. As we finished our meal, Hooshi offered dessert, but I declined, feeling stuffed. Leaving the restaurant, Hooshi opened the car door, and as we headed to my house, I couldn't help but smile at her. The spark I felt was intense, and I didn't want to look away, though I tried not to seem overly captivated.

CHAPTER

3

AWAKENING TO A NEW DAY: BREAKFAST AND BLOOD

Arriving home, Hooshi let me out, and our eyes met again, exchanging smiles. Nervously, Hooshi agreed to come inside, sensing something unexplainable in me that intrigued her. In the cozy living room, Mary and I enjoyed each other's company, cuddling while watching a movie. As the night progressed, I fell asleep with Mary resting on my chest. Waking up at midnight, I realized the time and urgently called my assistant. He arrived, and together we gently moved Mary upstairs to bed. Concerned, my assistant questioned if it was a good idea, but I assured him that Mary was special. The next morning, Mary woke up with a smile, cooked breakfast, and decided to call me. To her surprise, a guy answered and informed her that I was there. Interrupting my unconventional activities, I took the call. Oblivious to the context, Mary invited me for breakfast, and I agreed, wrapping up my task with Windle, my assistant. As I drove to Mary's house, Windle sat in the back, unaware of the ongoing war with gangs. I, the head of the snake, had started the conflict by eliminating the rival gang's leader. Arriving at Mary's house, I greeted her warmly, and we shared a hug. Mary prepared breakfast, and I expressed my love for pancakes. She suggested adding blueberries or chocolate chips next time, a thought that pleased me. As I reach for the cup of orange juice, Mary notices the blood on my sleeve. Nervous, I try to downplay it, telling Mary it's just blood. Frustrated, Mary questions why I had to shoot someone before coming to see her. I reassure her, apologizing and promising it won't happen again. While Mary cleans a plate, I ask about her plans for the day and suggest spending time together. However, Mary, still upset about the blood, requests that I not come around with blood on my clothing. I stand up, apologize again, and take over the dishwashing. Mary turns to me, asking if I'm okay, and I respond that I have to be. Desiring a connection, Mary wishes for a kiss, but I walk away, suggesting we leave. The unspoken love between us grows, though Hooshi, living a dangerous life since she was 12, struggles with the romantic aspects of her life. Past relationships often didn't work due to her lifestyle, but with Mary, there seems to be a unique connection that Hooshi values more than anything she has experienced before.

4

UNRAVELING SECRETS: MARY'S DETERMINATION TO KNOW

In the vibrant casino, Mary and I decided to try our luck at blackjack. Confident in our skills, we turned $2,000 into chips, ready for an exciting game. The tables were lively, and we were thoroughly enjoying ourselves until a rude guy bumped into me without an apology. Hooshi, my fiery protector, confronted him, leading to a fight that got broken up by Windle. Distressed, Mary slapped me for not heeding her request about the blood. As we walked away, Mary expressed her dissatisfaction with how I handled the situation. Surprised, I questioned if that was the reason for the slap, but she clarified it was about the blood. I couldn't help but laugh, appreciating the quirky dynamics of our relationship. Mary insisted on the no-blood rule, emphasizing it as true love. We discussed introducing Windle, and Mary suggested he drive us back to her house. Windle opened the back door, and as we continued our journey, there was a mix of tension and connection between us. As we arrived at my house, I invited Hooshi in, but she mentioned having something to handle. Refusing to be left behind, I insisted on accompanying her. Windle, sharing a look with Hooshi, didn't object. In the car, Hooshi instructed me to stay put when we reached a graffiti-covered apartment complex. Although nervous, I assured her I was fine. Hooshi and Windle left the car, disappearing into a store. From my vantage point, I couldn't see what unfolded inside. The tension built as I waited, wondering about the nature of Hooshi's business. I sensed the gravity of what lay behind that door – a disturbing scene of confined women, drug paraphernalia, weapons, and scattered money. The reality of Hooshi's world became starkly evident, leaving me with mixed emotions and a desire to understand the complexities she navigated. As the tense scene unfolded, I noticed a worker sleeping, and I woke him with a swift slap. Furious at the lapse in responsibility, I yelled and took matters into my own hands, pistol-whipping the negligent guy. I instructed him to find a partner for rotating shifts, despite the bleeding, and ordered him to clean up. Windle, with a duffle bag for my money, played his part in this covert operation. In the midst of chaos, I quickly snorted a line of coke. Amidst the commotion, I heard a noise and rushed to the front to prevent anyone from approaching the exposed area where the women were kept. To my surprise, it was Mary at the door, wondering why I was taking so long. The unexpected encounter added another layer of complexity to the unfolding situation, leaving her anxious and curious about what was happening inside. Finally, I mustered the courage to explain. "Mary, someone fell asleep on the job, and we needed to collect some money." But her keen eyes saw through my facade, and she insisted on coming inside to see for herself. My heart raced as Windle finally arrived with the bag of money, offering a small sense of relief. However, Mary's determination only grew stronger. She demanded to know what was really going on, refusing to accept anything less than the truth. I stood there, silent and conflicted, unsure of how much to reveal. As Mary stepped inside, I felt a surge of anxiety. I knew she was about to witness something she wasn't prepared for. Inside, the scene was grim – confined women, stacked weapons, and the money Windle had left. The sight made my stomach churn, and I couldn't bear to meet Mary's gaze. When a worker with a busted nose looked at Mary and then at me with confusion, I knew I had to act. I signaled for Mary to let me handle it, hoping to shield her from the harsh reality of my world. But her insistence on knowing the truth weighed heavily on me. As we left the scene behind, Mary's questions lingered in the air. She wanted to understand, to make sense of the darkness she had glimpsed. Reluctantly, I began to explain, revealing the truth about the women we had seen – bought and sold like commodities in a cruel and unforgiving world. It was a truth I had tried to shield her from, but one that she deserved to know. They come here with needle marks already on them; they don't get that here, but food, water, and clothes," I continued to explain. Mary started to cry, then asked, "what is the coke for?" "I have people bag it up, and it gets shipped out for distribution," I answered. Mary walked out in tears, and I flipped the table in anger, grabbing a brick of coke; Windal followed behind. I went to open the door for Mary, but she was not with it; she walked around the car and opened the door herself to get in. On the drive back, there was no talking, complete silence. Mary didn't understand what I meant that night at the restaurant until now. She tried to find a way to forgive me, but she respected me for not lying to her. She was confused about why I was so truthful with her. "Does that make me different from all the rest?" She became self-conscious of herself, as if there was something wrong with her. So when the car stopped, Mary got out; I followed behind her, saying "Mary" out loud. She kept walking, finally stopping at the door, Windal sitting in the car playing music out of respect for me. Mary asked me "why did you ask me for dinner?" The lifestyle I had, I wanted someone to have, to take me away from the lifestyle I grew up knowing, and eventually, the responsibility was passed down to me. I accepted myself and loved myself; I wanted someone who could do the same.

CHAPTER

5

ALONE IN THE DARKNESS: HOOSHI'S MOMENT OF RECKONING

Hooshi's heartfelt explanation left me stunned, grappling with a mix of emotions—anger, sadness, frustration, fear, and confusion. As I stood there, contemplating, Hooshi remained outside, waiting for a response. I couldn't decide whether to let her in or not. Part of me wanted to forgive her, but another part urged me not to make it too easy. If what Hooshi said was true, she would come back. Eventually, I retreated upstairs, leaving Hooshi outside to ponder her actions. Windal took her home, and she found herself alone, surrounded by guards in her fortified house. As she sat at her bar, pouring herself a drink and lighting a cigarette, she couldn't shake the paranoia that plagued her. Mary didn't deserve to live in constant fear, she realized. In frustration, Hooshi dismissed her guards, but they hesitated, sensing something was wrong. Windal, concerned, questioned her, prompting Hooshi to confront the turmoil within herself. With a pistol in front of her, Hooshi sat in silence, grappling with the weight of her decisions. As I sit with Windal in my home, contemplating the tumultuous events of the day, my mind races with thoughts of Mary. Her unexpected intrusion into my world has left me feeling vulnerable and exposed, yet strangely hopeful. Windal's presence provides a sense of comfort as I grapple with the weight of my emotions. Mary's reaction to discovering the truth about my illicit activities has left me reeling. Despite my efforts to shield her from the darkness of my world, she stumbled upon the grim reality of my existence. The tears in her eyes as she witnessed the suffering of those women shook me to my core, forcing me to confront the harsh reality of my choices.

CHAPTER

6

REFLECTIONS IN THE DARK

As I sip on my whiskey and light another cigarette, I find myself questioning the nature of my relationship with Mary. Her unwavering curiosity and genuine concern for my well-being stand in stark contrast to the superficial connections I've experienced in the past. There's something about Mary that draws me in, compelling me to open up in ways I never thought possible. I confide in Windal about my conflicting emotions, admitting my fear of losing Mary yet recognizing the necessity of protecting her from the dangers of my world. Despite my desire to shield her from harm, I can't deny the undeniable bond that has formed between us. As I contemplate stepping away from my life of crime, I feel a sense of relief wash over me. Entrusting Windal with the future of our operation, I am filled with a newfound sense of purpose. It's time to leave behind the shadows and embrace the light, guided by my love for Mary and a desire for redemption. Windal's words of encouragement and pride bring a swell of emotion to my chest. His unwavering support and belief in my decision to choose love over my criminal lifestyle fill me with a sense of validation and purpose. As we drive to Mary's house, I feel a mix of apprehension and determination. Windal's presence provides a steady anchor amidst the storm of uncertainty swirling within me. Arriving at Mary's house, I find myself paralyzed with indecision. Peering through the window, I catch a glimpse of Mary, her expression unreadable. Doubt gnaws at me, urging me to turn away and spare her the pain of my presence. Yet, a glimmer of hope flickers within me, urging me to take a chance and seek forgiveness. Summoning every ounce of courage, I lift my hand and knock on the door. The sound reverberates through the quiet night, echoing my inner turmoil. When Mary opens the door, I am met with a mixture of relief and trepidation. Her gaze pierces through me, and for a moment, I fear she will turn me away. But then, she speaks, her voice soft yet tinged with uncertainty. In that moment, I see a spark of forgiveness in her eyes, a willingness to give me another chance. The weight of her acceptance washes over me, and I step inside, grateful for the opportunity to make amends. As I stand before Mary, I am acutely aware of the distance that still lies between us. Yet, I am determined to bridge that gap, to prove to her that I am worthy of her love and trust. Taking a deep breath, I meet her gaze and offer a tentative smile, hoping that she can see the sincerity in my eyes. Mary's abrupt interruption catches me off guard, but her direct question demands an immediate response. "I've been taking care of some business," I reply, my voice tinged with weariness. Mary's concern about my appearance doesn't escape her notice, and I can't help but feel a pang of guilt for causing her worry. Her reaction to my explanation is a mix of surprise and disappointment, and I can't blame her for feeling that way. I had hoped to shield her from the darker aspects of my life, but now the truth lay bare before her. As I plead for her understanding and promise a better future, Mary's silence hangs heavy in the air. My heart pounds with uncertainty, fearing that I've lost her for good. But then, after what feels like an eternity, she finally speaks one simple word: "Okay." Relief floods through me, mingled with gratitude and hope. With renewed determination, I rise to my feet, eager to set my plans in motion and make good on my promise to Mary. Leaving her with a promise to return, I step out into the night, my mind racing with thoughts of the future we could build together. But fate has other plans, and before I know it, the world comes crashing down around me. The sound of a gunshot shatters the silence, and I feel a searing pain in my neck. Blood gushes from the wound as I struggle to comprehend what's happening. In the chaos that ensues, Windal's voice cuts through the panic, offering reassurance and support. As darkness threatens to engulf me, I cling to his words, finding solace in the promise of his unwavering loyalty. Despite the uncertainty of what lies ahead, I draw strength from the knowledge that I am not alone in this moment of crisis.

As I sit here, my mind is clouded with the events of the past few days. Mary's face flashes before my eyes, her laughter echoing in my ears. But alongside those memories are the darker ones, the ones I tried to shield her from, the ones that led to this moment. I can't shake the feeling of regret, of wishing I could go back and change things, make different choices that would have kept her safe from the darkness that lurked in my world. But I can't change the past, no matter how much I wish I could. Windal's words ring in my ears, his broken voice pleading with me to hold on, to fight for my life. But I know deep down that my time has come, that I can't escape the fate that awaits me. Despite the pain, despite the sorrow, I find a strange sense of peace knowing that I experienced true love, even if it was only for a fleeting moment. Mary's love was a beacon of light in the darkness of my life, and for that, I am grateful. As I slip away, I find comfort in the knowledge that Mary will be safe, that she will find happiness even in the midst of her grief. And as I take my final breath, I whisper a silent goodbye, knowing that my legacy will live on in the hearts of those who loved me. As anger simmers beneath the surface, Windal knows that breaking the news to Mary will only cause her pain. As he enters her house, she senses something is wrong, his presence heavy with grief. Her heart pounding in her chest as she watched him approach, his appearance shocking her to the core. "Windal, where is Hooshi?" I ask, my voice trembling with fear. His own grief is evident in every syllable. Despite his efforts to remain composed, tears stream down his cheeks, and I can see the anguish etched into his expression. But his response is silence, his body collapsing to the floor in a wave of anguish. My world crumbles around me as I realize the truth, and I rush outside, desperate to find Hooshi, to shake her awake from this nightmare. But as I hold her lifeless body in my arms, the weight of reality crashes down upon me, and I am consumed with grief. Windal's words pierce through the fog of despair, urging me to leave this place of sorrow behind. With a heavy heart, I climb into the car, the pain of loss weighing me down as we drive away from the life we once knew. As Windal drives, his mind races with thoughts of vengeance and justice for Hooshi's untimely death. The weight of grief and anger hangs heavy in the air, his emotions roiling with each passing moment. As he continues to weep, I reach out to him, offering what little comfort I can in this moment of profound loss. His sorrow is palpable, a testament to the deep bond he shared with Hooshi, a bond forged in loyalty and love. Hooshi's words echo in my mind, her acceptance of fate and her gratitude for experiencing true love. I can't help but feel a sense of emptiness, knowing that she is gone, that the future we had dreamed of together will never come to pass.

CHAPTER

7

IN THE SHADOW OF LOSS:
FINDING PURPOSE IN GRIEF

Arriving at Hooshi's father's house, Windal is met with a mix of emotions—anger, sadness, and determination. He knows that Hooshi's father shares his desire for retribution, his grief mirroring Windal's own. "Don't worry," Hooshi's father assures him, his voice filled with conviction. "These people will pay for what they've done." In that moment, Windal finds solace in the shared resolve to seek justice for Hooshi's death. Together, they vow to bring those responsible to account, no matter the cost. With a renewed sense of purpose, Windal sets out to fulfill his promise to Hooshi, determined to honor her memory and ensure that her legacy lives on. Mary listens to Hooshi's father's words, feeling a mix of emotions swirling within her. Despite the pain of losing Hooshi, she finds solace in the wisdom and compassion of her father-in-law. She takes a deep breath, trying to steady herself amidst the turmoil of grief and confusion. As she looks into her father-in-law's eyes, she sees a reflection of Hooshi's love and strength, a reminder of the bond they shared. With a nod, Mary acknowledges his words, silently promising to honor Hooshi's memory and the love they shared. She knows that moving forward won't be easy, but she also knows that she carries a piece of Hooshi with her, a guiding light to navigate the darkness. Together, they stand in silent solidarity, bound by their love for Hooshi and their determination to keep her spirit alive in their hearts.

Legacy of Love: Embracing Hope in the Darkness

As Mary reflects on her journey, she realizes that while the pain of losing Hooshi will never fully fade, she has found a sense of peace and purpose in carrying on her legacy. She knows that Hooshi would want her to live her life to the fullest, embracing each day with courage and resilience.

With the support of Hooshi's father and Windal, Mary finds the strength to face the challenges ahead. Together, they work tirelessly to uncover the truth behind Hooshi's death and bring those responsible to justice.

Despite the darkness that once threatened to consume her, Mary emerges stronger and more determined than ever. She continues to honor Hooshi's memory by living with kindness, compassion, and unwavering love.

And though their time together was tragically cut short, Mary finds solace in the knowledge that the love she shared with Hooshi will always endure, lighting the way forward even in the darkest of times.

Love isn't guaranteed; it's what you make of it, whether dead or alive. This story is about being true to yourself and not giving up on the light you see, no matter how hard life gets. It will always be there, waiting for you. Love to everybody! Stay creative, my butterfly! Let your light shine!

www.ingramcontent.com/pod-product-compliance
Lightning Source LLC
Chambersburg PA
CBHW020346130626
46549CB00003B/1312